MR MAJEIKA'S POSTBAG

Humphrey Carpenter is well known as a writer and has published biographies of Tolkien, C. S. Lewis, W. H. Auden and most recently, Benjamin Britten as well as his *Oxford Companion to Children's Literature*. His children's books include several about Mr Majeika, all published in Puffin. He lives in Oxford with his wife and two daughters.

By the same author

MR MAJEIKA
MR MAJEIKA AND THE MUSIC TEACHER
MR MAJEIKA AND THE HAUNTED HOTEL
MR MAJEIKA AND THE DINNER LADY
MR MAJEIKA AND THE SCHOOL PLAY
MR MAJEIKA AND THE SCHOOL INSPECTOR
MR MAJEIKA AND THE SCHOOL BOOK WEEK

HUMPHREY CARPENTER

MR MAJEIKA'S POSTBAG

Illustrated by Robin Kingsland

Based on scripts by Jenny McDade

PUFFIN BOOKS

PUFFIN BOOKS

Published by the Penguin Group
Penguin Books Ltd, 27 Wrights Lane, London W8 5TZ, England
Penguin Books USA Inc., 375 Hudson Street, New York, New York 10014, USA
Penguin Books Australia Ltd, Ringwood, Victoria, Australia
Penguin Books Canada Ltd, 10 Alcorn Avenue, Toronto, Ontario, Canada M4V 3B2
Penguin Books (NZ) Ltd, 182–190 Wairau Road, Auckland 10, New Zealand

Penguin Books Ltd, Registered Offices: Harmondsworth, Middlesex, England

First published by Fantail Books 1990
Published in Puffin Books 1994
1 3 5 7 9 10 8 6 4 2

Typeset by Datix International Limited, Bungay, Suffolk
Printed in England by Clays Ltd, St Ives plc

Contents

The not-so-little mermaid

'Rules are rules,' said the Worshipful Wizard firmly, 'and wishes are wishes, especially magical ones made by wizards, and my final word on the subject, Wilhelmina Worlock, is *no*.'

Miss Worlock, the fat old witch who had been trying to marry Mr Majeika for years and years and years, dabbed at her eyes with a black lace handkerchief. 'Just ones more times, Your Worshipfulness,' she pleaded. 'Just ones more times. I'm sure he didn't means it.'

'You know very well he meant it,' said the Worshipful Wizard. 'It was on the day of his birthday, and I heard him say, very clearly "I wish not to see Wilhelmina Worlock again for a very long time."'

'Cruels, cruels,' sobbed Wilhelmina.

'A wish is a wish, Wilhelmina,' said the Worshipful Wizard severely. 'The rule is, never to go against a magical wish made by a wizard. In any case, you've already broken it once – when you went down to Britland and tried to marry him disguised as Myrtle Bindweed.'

'I knows,' sobbed Willy Worlock, 'and I'm truly sorrys. But, your Worshipfulness, love is a many-splendoured things, and I've got to see him again, or my heart will breaks.' She squeezed out her sopping handkerchief all over the tiny wizard who guarded the trapdoor that led down to Britland.

'Oy!' protested the tiny wizard.

'Now listen here, Wilhelmina,' said the Worshipful Wizard sternly. 'You're not to go down to Britland again – I don't want Majeika to be pestered by you.' He turned to the tiny wizard. 'Don't in any circumstances let her through the trapdoor,' he told him.

'You bet I won't Your Worshipfulness,' said the tiny wizard. 'You bet I won't.'

A few hours later, the tiny wizard was dozing

by the trapdoor, when somebody nudged him
awake. 'Here,' said a voice, 'open ups.'

The tiny wizard blinked sleepily. 'Who are
you, then?' he enquired suspiciously. 'Ain't seen
you around here before. You sure you got
permission to go down?'

'Course I has,' said the voice. It belonged, the
tiny wizard now saw, to an enormous mermaid.

She was very fat, and she had a fish's tail
that would have been too big for any
fishmonger's slab. She had long golden hair, as
all mermaids do, but it looked suspiciously like
a wig, and she was wearing dark glasses. 'Get

on with its,' she hissed, pushing the tiny wizard aside and opening the trapdoor.

'Oy,' yelled the tiny wizard. 'Stop that! You can't fool me with that disguise. I know who you are!

But the mermaid had already pushed the trapdoor open and jumped through.

It was a lovely sunny afternoon, and Mr Potter, the headmaster of St Barty's was fishing on the banks of Barty Brook. He hadn't had a bite all day, and he was just dozing off when he felt his rod jerking violently.

He grabbed hold of the rod, and started to reel in the line. But it wasn't a fish that appeared from the water. The hook was caught in the yellow hair of some enormous creature that was rising from the depths.

'Yoo hoo!' called a voice from beneath the tangled hair. 'Yoo hoo! Mr Pottys!'

Mr Potter blinked. 'A mermaid,' he gasped. 'A mermaid with the voice of Wilhelmina Worlock!'

The line broke and he fell over on his back. When he sat up again, the mermaid had vanished.

'I said breast-stroke, Thomas Grey, not doggie-paddle!' roared Mrs Bunty Brace-Girdle. At the Barty Baths, Thomas was being given a swimming lesson. He hated every minute of it.

Melanie was an excellent swimmer, but Thomas had never managed to learn properly, and now Melanie's mother had been appointed Swimming Instructress at St Barty's School, so she was making it her business to teach him. She'd been giving him lessons every day for a month, but he wasn't getting any better.

'Come along, *I'll* show you,' said Mrs Brace-Girdle, and she plunged into the water and began thrashing about.

Thomas watched her and sighed. 'Somehow,' he said to Melanie, 'I don't think I'm ever going to get the hang of this.'

'Yes, Majeika,' said Mr Potter cheerily at the beginning of school on Monday morning, 'tomorrow it's our annual Seaside Expedition.'

'Did you say Seaside, Mr Potter?' asked Mr Majeika nervously. 'What sort of things do Britlanders do at the seaside?'

'Well, Majeika,' said Mr Potter, 'You need to bring a bucket and spade, so that you can build sandcastles.'

'Ah,' said Mr Majeika sounding relieved. 'Is that all?'

'Oh, there's lots of other things to do,' said Mr Potter. 'You can collect shells, and buy ice-

creams, and ride on the roundabouts, and eat
fish and chips.'

'That sounds very nice, Mr Potter,' said Mr
Majeika.

'And of course,' said Mr Potter, 'We'll all go
paddling.'

'Paddling?' said Mr Majeika turning pale.
'You mean — in the water?'

Mr Potter nodded. 'That's the best thing
about the seaside, Majeika. To take off your

shoes and socks, and feel the sand between
your toes, and then go running into the water,
and feel the waves washing around your ankles.
I just can't wait! . . . I say, Majeika, are you
feeling all right?'

*

'You see,' Mr Majeika explained to Melanie
and Thomas, 'Walpurgians have this problem.
They mustn't let water touch their feet, or — '

'Don't tell me, Mr Majeika,' said Thomas,
'let me guess . . . They turn into mermaids?'

Mr Majeika nodded. 'Well, in my case it
would be a mer*man*. But however did you
guess, Thomas?'

'It's the sort of thing that *would* happen in
Walpurgis,' said Thomas.

'But would you mind being a merman, Mr
Majeika?' asked Melanie. 'I'd have thought it
would be fun.'

Mr Majeika shuddered. 'Would you want to
spend the rest of your life with a fish-tail

15

instead of legs, never being able to walk on dry land again, and having to marry the first mermaid you see?'

'Marry the first mermaid you see?' asked Melanie. 'Is that the rule?'

Mr Majeika nodded gloomily. 'I'm afraid it is, Melanie. So you see, when we get to the seaside, I'm going to have to find an excuse not to go anywhere near the water.'

'Time to take off your shoes and socks,
everyone!' called Mr Potter from the beach.
'Time to go paddling!' They had all arrived in
the coach. As usual, Hamish Bigmore had been
rude to the driver all the way except when the
bus had stopped for him to be sick; but
somehow they had got there.

'Oh, Mr Potter, please don't let's paddle
quite yet,' called Mr Majeika nervously from
the promenade. Thomas and Melanie could see
that he was keeping as far from the water's
edge as possible. 'Couldn't we make sandcastles
first? I've brought my bucket and spade, just
like you said.'

'Ah, so I see, Majeika,' said Mr Potter, eyeing

the enormous household bucket and big garden spade that Mr Majeika was carrying. 'They're not quite what I had in mind, but I suppose they'll do. All right, everyone, we'll start with the sandcastle competition. I'll come back and judge your castles in half an hour. Meanwhile I'm off for a bit of quiet fishing from the pier.'

Twenty minutes later, Thomas and Melanie had finished building a lovely sandcastle, complete with turrets and battlements and a drawbridge and moat. 'My isn't that wonderful,' said Mr Majeika when they showed it to him. 'I'm sure you'll win the prize when Mr Potter comes back to do the judging.'

At that moment, there was a roaring noise behind them. Hamish Bigmore was pretending that he was riding a powerful motorbike: **'Vroom, vroom, vroooooooooooom.'** He roared past them – slap into the middle of the sandcastle. When he got up and dusted the sand off himself, Thomas and Melanie could see that nothing of the castle was left. 'Why, you — ' said Thomas, lunging out at Hamish. But before he could reach him, Mr Majeika flicked his tuft of hair — which meant that magic was on the way — and there was a flash and a puff of smoke, and the sound of trumpets.

Melanie and Thomas looked around them. The beach and the sea had vanished, and they were sitting on huge carved chairs in a big hall. Nevertheless there was something familiar about the place. 'Look, Thomas,' said Melanie, 'the whole place is built of sand.'

'Yes, Melanie! It's our sandcastle, grown big, and we're inside it! And look at our clothes.'

They realised that they were dressed as a king and queen.

At that moment there was a roll of drums, and the doors at the far end of the hall opened to reveal Mr Majeika leading in Hamish Bigmore.

'Your Majesties,' called Mr Majeika, 'I have the miscreant Bigmore as prisoner, he who attempted to destroy your castle. What dreadful punishment shall you mete out to him?'

Thomas and Melanie looked at each other and giggled. 'Have you got any ideas, Mr Majeika?' asked Melanie.

Mr Majeika thought for a moment. 'Well, your Majesties, there is a fairground a short way from this castle, and in that fairground is a Ghost Train. Maybe . . . ?'

'What a good idea,' said Thomas. 'Hamish Bigmore, we sentence you to ride on the Ghost Train.'

'Ghost Train!' scoffed Hamish. 'What a silly babyish thing. As if I'd be frightened by *that*.'

But once again Mr Majeika wiggled his tuft of hair, and there was another flash and puff of smoke, and suddenly they were all riding on the Ghost Train, Hamish in the open carriage in front of them. And it was very dark, and when they

went round a corner Hamish screamed, because
Mr Majeika had arranged it that, just for once,
the Ghost Train should have real ghosts in it ...

*

'Ah, there you are, Majeika,' said Mr Potter,
returning to the beach with his fishing tackle
under his arm. 'Didn't catch anything, alas. And
do you know, for the second time this week, I
thought I saw a mermaid. Must have been
something I ate.'

'A mermaid, Mr Potter?' said Mr Majeika

looking down worriedly at his feet, to make sure he hadn't got them wet and already begun to grow a fish-tail himself. 'Oh, Mr Potter, I'm sure you must be mistaken.'

'I expect I was, Majeika. Anyway, now it's time for paddling. Get those shoes and socks off, and take the children into the water!'

'Oh, but Mr Potter,' said Mr Majeika desperately, 'you haven't judged the sandcastle competition.'

'Time's getting on, Majeika, and we can skip the judging. After all, there's no point in coming to the sea if you don't go into the water.'

'I suppose not, Mr Potter,' said Mr Majeika miserably, beginning to take off his shoes and socks, 'But couldn't the children go paddling by themselves?'

'There must be a grown-up to supervise them,' said Mr Potter firmly. 'After all, you sometimes find strange things in the water, like jellyfish. And mermaids,' he added thoughtfully.

'Anyway, Majeika, it'll have to be you, because I'm going to do some more fishing.'

At that moment, a brisk voice called across the beach. 'Mr Potter! Mr Potter!'

'My goodness,' said Mr Potter, 'Bunty Brace-Girdle! Whatever are you doing here?'

'It was such a lovely day,' explained Mrs Brace-Girdle, when she had caught up with them, 'that I thought I'd pop over to Barty Bay in the motor, and make sure that these youngsters get some swimming practice. In particular Thomas Grey, who's still got a lot to learn in the water.'

'Oh, please, no swimming, Mrs Brace-Girdle,' said Thomas. 'I'm getting on all right in the swimming baths, but these waves frighten me.' He pointed out to sea; certainly the waves were rough today. 'I'll paddle, but please don't make me swim.'

'Nonsense,' said Bunty Brace-Girdle firmly. 'You'll find the salt-water helps to keep you afloat,

Thomas. Here, I've brought your swimming things. 'And she threw Thomas's towel and bathing costume over to him. Miserably, he went behind a rock and began to change.

'Mummy,' said Melanie, 'if you're here, Mr Majeika doesn't need to come into the water, does he?'

'Of course not,' snapped Mrs Brace-Girdle. 'In fact, I'd be greatly obliged if he stayed well away from it. I've got enough trouble looking after Thomas Grey without having to cope with *him*.'

Twenty minutes later, Melanie and Mr Majeika were happily gathering shells from the edge of a rock-pool. Mrs Brace-Girdle had forgotten all about Melanie in her determination to get Thomas into the water, so Melanie had managed to slip away.

'So you didn't have to turn into a merman after all, Mr Majeika,' said Melanie. 'And now there's a storm getting up, so I expect we'll all be going home soon. Look, even the surface of this pool is getting quite ruffled by the wind.'

The water in the pool was indeed beginning to pitch and toss, but it wasn't the wind that was disturbing it. Something was coming up from the depths. There was a great bubbling sound, and suddenly a huge head of dripping yellow hair thrust itself out and grinned at Mr Majeika.

'Yoo-hoo!' it cried. 'My Majeikas!'

'Oh no!' gasped Mr Majeika. 'Wilhelmina Worlock!'

The mermaid shook her head. 'Yous must be mistakens, pretty boy,' she said. 'I is Medusa the Mermaid, a Walpurgian Water-Sprite. So why don't you come down and see me sometimes?' With which, she vanished again beneath the surface of the pool.

Mr Majeika was breathing hard. 'I'm sure it was Wilhelmina Worlock,' he said anxiously.

'Of course it was,' said Melanie. 'I'd know

that voice — and that shape — anywhere. Still, Mr Majeika, if she's really turned into a mermaid, she won't be able to walk about on dry land, and you can escape from her easily enough.'

'I suppose so,' said Mr Majeika gloomily. 'But whatever happens, I must keep my feet dry!'

*

When Melanie and Mr Majeika got back to the others, they found Melanie's mother looking worried.

'I can't see Thomas,' she was saying. 'He was swimming quite well — he got out as far as that rock. But he's suddenly vanished. I'd better go in myself, and have a look for him. Is there somewhere I can change?' For Mrs Brace-Girdle was still in her clothes.

'You can undress behind that rock there, Mummy,' said Melanie. 'But do hurry.' She anxiously scanned the sea while her mother went off to put on her bathing costume. 'Oh, I think I can see him — he's bobbing about a long way away. And he looks as if he's in difficulties. *I'm* not waiting to change, Mr Majeika — I'm going to rescue him.' Pulling off her shoes and socks, Melanie ran into the sea.

Mr Majeika watched her anxiously. 'Oh dear, oh dear,' he muttered. 'If only I dared go into the water myself. Maybe I could try a spell to make the sea calmer.' He flicked his tuft of hair, but it had the opposite effect. The wind began to roar and the sea became rougher than ever. 'Oh dear,' said Mr Majeika. 'Wrong spell.'

Mrs Brace-Girdle emerged from behind the rock, in her swimming costume. 'Where's

Melanie?' she asked. Mr Majeika told her what had happened. 'Bother,' she said. 'The sea is getting very rough. At this rate I shall have *two* children to rescue.'

The sea was indeed rough by the time Melanie got near enough to see Thomas clearly. His head kept going beneath the water, and he was spluttering and waving his arms in panic. 'I'm coming, Thomas!' she yelled, but her voice couldn't be heard above the storm, and then a big wave came and swamped her so that for a few moments all she could see was water.

When the wave had passed, there was only the empty sea, and no sign of Thomas. 'Help!'

called Melanie. 'Mummy! Mr Majeika! Thomas is drowning!'

Mrs Brace-Girdle was swimming out from the shore, but she could only make slow progress against the stormy sea. Suddenly someone rushed down the beach and plunged into the waves. A kind of rocket seemed to zoom across the surface of the water, and in a moment Mr Majeika, still in his clothes, had surfaced beside Melanie. 'Where is he?' he gasped. 'Where's Thomas?'

'Oh, Mr Majeika, I don't know,' spluttered Melanie. 'He was over there until a wave came and covered me.' Mr Majeika plunged in the direction Melanie had pointed, went beneath the water, and a moment later had come up again, carrying a dripping shape. 'You've done it!' called Melanie. 'You've rescued him! Is he all right?'

'He'll be all right,' called Mr Majeika. 'But he's too heavy to carry back to the shore. I'll

have to teach him how to swim.' And he
wiggled his tuft of hair.

*

Mrs Brace-Girdle had struggled back to the
shore; the waves were too much for her. She
lay panting for breath at the edge of the water,
anxiously looking out to sea. Suddenly she saw
a figure swimming powerfully to shore. It was
Thomas Grey.

'Good grief!' called Mrs Brace-Girdle. 'You
seem to have become a champion swimmer
in a jiffy, Thomas. Quite a magical
transformation.'

Wiping the salt-water from his eyes, Thomas

nodded. 'Quite magical, Mrs Brace-Girdle,' he said.

'It was very brave of you, Mr Majeika,' said Melanie, as they swam to the shore together. 'We must get you a nice hot cup of tea to warm you up again.' She could see that he was shivering.

'No tea for me, I'm afraid, Melanie,' said Mr Majeika miserably. 'In fact, I mustn't let your mother, or Mr Potter, or any Britlanders see me at all. I've got to stay here now, you know.'

'Oh!' said Melanie, who had quite forgotten. She looked behind, at where his legs ought to be thrashing the water. Sure enough she saw,

instead of legs or feet, a large fish tail. 'Oh dear, poor Mr Majeika,' she said. 'You really have turned into a merman.'

'And that's not all,' said Mr Majeika. 'Don't you remember . . . the first mermaid I see . . .?'

'You'll have to marry her! And, Mr Majeika, we know who it'll be, don't we?'

As if in answer came a voice from the rock-pool. 'Yoo-hoo! My Majeikas! Kissy Kissy!'

Mr Majeika covered his eyes. 'Oh no,' he gasped. 'I'd rather marry a sea-monster!'

Then suddenly there was a voice in his ear. **'Good afternoon, Majeika, sorry to trouble you, but we have a slight problem up here.'**

'Good afternoon, sir,' said Mr Majeika. ('It's the Worshipful Wizard talking to me from Walpurgis,' he explained to Melanie.)

'A certain member of our wizards' community has escaped without the proper permission,' explained the Worshipful Wizard. **'Miss Wilhelmina Worlock has barged**

through the Britland Trapdoor entirely contrary to instructions, crudely disguised as a mermaid. You don't happen to have spotted her, do you, Majeika?'

'Indeed I have, sir,' said Mr Majeika. 'I've got her in my sights right now. But you say "disguised as a mermaid", sir? Isn't she a real mermaid?'

'Certainly not, Majeika. She pinched a mermaid costume from the Wizards' pantomime rehearsal – they're doing "The Little Mermaid" for the next Christmas production.'

'A false fish tail, sir?'

'Exactly, Majeika.'

'So a wizard who happened to get turned into a merman wouldn't – wouldn't have to marry her?'

'Certainly not, Majeika. Why do you ask? Not in that situation yourself, I hope?'

'I'm afraid so, sir. Bit of a fishy business, you

might say. So I suppose I'm stuck this way, aren't I? As a merman?'

'**Not at all, Majeika. Even if you are a Failed Wizard, Third Class, you ought not to be so ignorant. Any well brought up Britland child knows that a mermaid, or a merman, who kisses a human being loses their fish tail and grows legs.**'

'Really, sir? So all I have to do is kiss a human, and be back to normal?'

'**That's right, Majeika. Glad to have sorted out that bit of bother. 'Bye for now.**'

'Oh, goodbye, sir, and thank you.'

At that moment, Mrs Brace-Girdle came swimming up to them. 'Thought I'd better plunge in,' she puffed, 'and make sure you two are all right. Why, Mr Majeika, whatever are you doing?'

'He's kissing you, Mummy,' explained Melanie, laughing.

'Well, I—!' spluttered Mrs Brace-Girdle.

'Don't worry, Mummy,' said Melanie. 'It's all in a good cause. There's nothing fishy about it, is there, Mr Majeika?'

'Not at all,' answered Mr Majeika, as they reached the shore and he walked out of the sea happily on his own legs. 'Sorry, Wilhelmina,' he called to the head that had risen once more out of the rock pool. 'It's back to Walpurgis with you, I'm afraid – as you can see, I've found my sea legs!'

'Oo,' grumbled Wilhelmina Worlock. 'It's not fairs, it really isn't. Aren't I nevers going to get my Majeikas in awful wedded bliss?' A black balloon floated down from Walpurgis, and, miserably, Wilhelmina took hold of the string and floated up again with it, back into the sky.

'Who's the parachutist?' asked Mr Potter, who had just arrived with his fishing tackle. 'Friend of yours, Majeika? Looked a bit like Miss Worlock. Ah well, the only thing I caught was an empty sardine tin. But I'll say this, a day at the seaside is wonderfully restful, isn't it, Majeika?'

'Oh yes, Mr Potter,' said Mr Majeika, sinking exhaustedly on to the beach. 'Wonderfully!'

Mr Majeika's postbag

Mr Majeika has been sending letters from Much
Barty to his Aunty Bubbles in Walpurgis, telling
her all about the goings-on at St Barty's School.
So that no Britlander should understand them,
he has been writing them in code – a different
code for each letter. See if you can work out
the code, and manage to read the letter!

20 8 5   23 9 14 4 13 9 12 12

13 21 3 8   2 1 18 20 25

10 21 12 25   20 8 5   6 9 18 19 20

4 5 11 8   1 21 14 20 25   2 21 2 21 12 5 19,

20 8 9 19   15 14 5   9 19   18 5 11 21 12 12 25   8 1 18 4.

9 14   6 13 20   9 20 19   19 15   8 11 18 4   9

3 11 14 20   23 18 9 20 5   1   12 15 14 7

12 5 20 20 5 18   9 14   9 20.

9   1 13   22 5 18 25   23 5 12 12,   1 14 4   9

8 15 16 5   25 15 21   1 18 5   20 15 15.   16 12 5 1 19 5

3 15 13 5   6 15 18   13 25   2 9 18 20 8 4 1 25.

6 18 15 13   25 15 21 18   12 15 22 9 14 7

14 5 16 8 5 23.

13 1 10 5 9 11 1.

P. S. If you can't understand this one, Aunty,
remember that there are twenty-six letters in
the Britland alphabet! Write them out with
their numbers beneath them, and see what
happens!

Eht Llimidniw
Hcum Ytrab
Yam eht ½2 (Naigruplaw Radnelac)

Read Ytnua Selbbub,
I ma gnisu a tnereffid edoc siht
emit esuaceb Samoht dna Einalem yas
eht tsal eno saw yerv ysae ot
dnatsrednu, os s'tel epoh eht wen
eno si ton os ysae, hguoht fo esruoc
I epoh **uoy** nac dear ti.
Ew evah neeb gnivah a Loohcs
Etef, hcihw saw taerg nuf, dna od
uoy wonk, I now eht puc rof Tseb
Naytrab, hcihw snaem eht tsom dnik
dna lufesu nosrep ni eht egalliv!
Samoht dna Einalem era gnimoc
dnuor noos ot knird regnig reeb
tuo fo ti.

      Morf ruoy gnivol wehpen,
      Akiejam.

D'you join Ken Peel?

'D'you ken John Peel with his coat so grey?'
sang Mr Potter, the headmaster of St Barty's,
as he galloped across the fields on horseback.
'D'you ken John Peel at the break of the day?
D'you ken John Peel when he's far away, With
his hounds and his horn in the morning?' It was
an old English hunting song, but Mr Majeika,
who was at his windmill, getting ready for
another day, was terrified out of his wits by
the distant sound. He was even more frightened
when Mr Potter, in a bright scarlet coat,
suddenly jumped over a hedge and appeared in
front of him, falling off his horse.

'Mr Potter!' he cried anxiously. 'Is this some
well-known Britland sport, falling off horses?
And why are you wearing red pyjamas?'

'These aren't pyjamas, Majeika,' said Mr
Potter crossly, getting up and brushing himself

down. 'This is Hunting Pink. It's what the Much Barty Hunt wears when it goes out for the day.'

'Goes out for the day?' repeated Mr Majeika. 'You mean a trip to the seaside, or something like that?'

'No, no, Majeika — when we go hunting. Ah,' said Mr Potter, warming to his subject, 'what a wonderful sight it is, Majeika. All of us on horseback in our Hunting Pink. Then the horn blows — tantivy! tantivy! — and we're up and away, over hill and down dale, until we've flushed the creature out of its hiding place, and then it's View Halloooo! and in go the hounds for the kill.'

'Goodness, Mr Potter,' said Mr Majeika, 'it does sound exciting. But what dreadful beast do you hunt? Is it some terrible fearsome thing with huge tusks and vast staring eyes, which will rip you to pieces if it catches you? Or maybe some gigantic poisonous snake that could surround the whole village and squeeze it tight?' He shuddered as he thought of some of the fearsome monsters that lurked in the outer darkness on the edge of Walpurgis, the land where the wizards come from.

'No, no, Majeika,' said Mr Potter irritably. 'It's a fox.'

'A fox, Mr Potter?' asked Mr Majeika, who still had a lot to learn about Britland. 'What's a fox?'

'Well,' said Mr Potter, 'it looks a bit like a dog with a long nose and a bushy tail.'

'So why do you chase it?' asked Mr Majeika puzzled. 'Is it terribly fierce, Mr Potter? Will it give you a savage bite if you go near it? Is it a danger to little children?'

'Not at all, Majeika. It'll run away the moment it sees you.'

'So what has it done wrong, Mr Potter, to make you chase it?' Mr Potter thought for a moment. 'It eats chickens, Majeika,' he said.

'But *I* eat chickens, Mr Potter,' said Mr Majeika, thoroughly puzzled. 'In fact, I had chicken for school dinner yesterday. And you didn't get on a horse and chase me just because of it. So I just don't understand why you're hunting the fox, Mr Potter.'

'Well,' said Mr Potter, 'you'd better come along and see for yourself, Majeika. The Much Barty Hunt meets tomorrow morning, outside the Barty Arms. I'm sure you'll enjoy yourself.'

'Now, come along Melanie,' snapped Melanie's mother, Mrs Bunty Brace-Girdle.

'Brush your hair properly before coming down to breakfast. Cousin Kenneth won't want to see a scruffy little girl.'

Melanie made a face. Cousin Kenneth was a horrid red-faced relation, the Honourable Kenneth Penshurst-Peel, who had come to stay in Much Barty to do some hunting. He claimed to be descended from the original John Peel, the famous huntsman in the song.

'I don't like Cousin Kenneth,' said Melanie. 'And I think hunting is cruel.'

'Nonsense, Melanie,' snapped her mother. 'It's a traditional English sport, and everyone knows that traditional English sports are what has made England so great. Anyway, all little girls like riding horses.'

'Yes, but not for chasing foxes. It's horrid.'

'Nonsense, Melanie,' said her mother firmly. 'I'm sure the fox loves every minute of it.'

'Come along, Hamish,' called Mrs Pamela

Bigmore, Hamish's mother. 'It's time to go off to the Hunt.' The Rolls Royce was standing ready in the Bigmores' front drive, but Hamish was nowhere to be seen.

'I'm not coming on the boring old hunt,' yelled a muffled voice from Hamish's bedroom. Hamish was still in bed, with the bedclothes pulled over his face.

'Oh, Hamie,' wailed his mother miserably. 'Just think of the lovely gee-gees you can look at, and the nice little doggies, and the pretty trees, just like the forests in those Tarzan films you love so much.'

The mention of Tarzan had given Hamish an idea. In his wardrobe was a Christmas present he hadn't yet used.

A few minutes later, something dark and furry came out of Hamish's bedroom and walked, on all fours, down the stairs. When Pam Bigmore saw it she gave a scream. 'King Kong!' she cried. 'A giant ape has got into my house and eaten my baby Hamish!'

'Don't be silly, Mum,' said Hamish's voice
from inside the creature's head. 'Don't you
remember this gorilla suit you gave me last
Christmas? You can follow the stupid old Hunt,
but *I'm* going into the wood, to swing about in
the trees and play Tarzan.'

Outside the Barty Arms, the members of the

Hunt were beginning to gather, on their horses.

'Ah, Mr Potter,' called Mrs Brace-Girdle, as the headmaster trotted up, 'may I introduce my cousin, the Honourable Kenneth Penshurst-Peel?'

'How do you do, Mr Honourable,' said Mr Potter vaguely, shaking hands with the red-faced Cousin Kenneth. 'Has anyone seen Majeika? I don't want him to be late for such an exciting event in the Much Barty calendar.'

'Majeika?' snorted Mrs Brace-Girdle. 'I can't think why you invited him, Mr Potter. Hunting is a serious business, isn't it, Cousin Kenneth?'

'Oh, fwightfully,' said Cousin Kenneth, stroking his moustache. 'A dweadfully sewious business. And I pwide myself on knowing more about the science of chasing the fox than most people, for my wemarkable ancestor was none other than – '

He was interrupted by a loud laugh from the rest of the Hunt. Angrily, he looked around to see who was laughing at him. But the laugh was directed at a curious figure which was approaching the Barty Arms on horseback.

Mr Majeika had managed to borrow a horse from Farmer Gurney, but it was very old and could only walk extremely slowly. Majeika had tried to get it to move a bit quicker by hanging a sugar lump from a pole in front of its nose. As to Hunting Pink, he had found a bright red wizard's costume in his chest of drawers, left over from some long-ago Walpurgian feast day, and had put that on, even though it was covered with the signs of the Zodiac. He had bought a riding-hat from a junk shop, but had cut a hole in the top of it, so that his tuft of hair could wiggle if he needed to do magic. But the oddest of all was the way he was riding.

'Why are you facing the horse's tail, Mr Majeika?' asked Thomas Grey, who had come up on his bike to watch the Hunt gathering. Mr Majeika was sitting back to front on the

horse, holding a fly-whisk to keep off the insects which buzzed around the animal's tail.

'Oh, this is how all Walpurgians ride, Thomas,' he answered. 'Don't Britlanders do the same?'

Thomas shook his head, and at that moment Mr Potter blew a hunting horn. Mr Majeika jumped with fright, and fell off the horse.

'I don't think this is your sort of thing at all, Mr Majeika,' said Thomas, as he helped him back on again.

'We have a slight problem,' called Mr Potter to the assembled members of the Hunt. 'Old Earl Barty, Our M.F.H., is not feeling very well today, and hasn't turned up. So would someone else please be today's M.F.H.?'

At once, Mr Majeika's hand shot up.

'You, Mr Majeika?' said Bunty Brace-Girdle scornfully. 'I'm surprised that you know what M.F.H. stands for.'

'Of course I do, Mrs Brace-Girdle,' said Mr Majeika eagerly. 'We have a M.F.H. each Wizards' Fun Day in Walpurgis — er, I mean, in the place I come from. It stands for Man in a Funny Hat. And I wasn't asking for the job myself. I suggest *him* — he's in a really funny hat.' He pointed at Cousin Kenneth.

Mrs Brace-Girdle went red in the face. 'Such impertinence!' she snorted. 'As every educated English person knows, M.F.H. stands for Master of Fox Hounds. And as for a funny hat, the gentleman you're pointing at is a very distinguished huntsman, the Honourable Kenneth, my cousin. He's descended from the famous huntsman John Peel, whose hat he's wearing.' Bunty indicated Cousin Kenneth's antique top hat. 'But you're quite right in one respect, Mr Majeika,' she went on. 'Who better than the Honourable Kenneth to lead our hunt? Tally ho, Cousin Kenneth!'

'Wight you are, Bunty!' responded Cousin Kenneth, striking his horse's flank with a riding-crop. And off rode the Hunt, with Melanie following on her pony, and Thomas on his bicycle – and Mr Majeika, owing to the fact that he was facing the horse's tail, going in the opposite direction for half a mile before he realized his mistake.

Pam Bigmore parked the Rolls Royce in a clearing in the wood, and got out a very expensive picnic hamper. 'I expect we'll see the nice gee-gees and the pretty doggies very easily from here, Hamie darling,' she said to Hamish.

Hamish did not answer. He was too busy being Tarzan. He sprang from the Rolls with a bloodcurdling cry of 'Woooooooooooooo!', causing Pam to drop the hamper in fright. Swinging on to a branch, he began to beat his chest: 'Woooooo! Woooooo!'

Half a mile away, the Barty Hounds pricked up their ears and changed direction. 'That's weally pwomising,' called Cousin Ken to Bunty. 'I weckon they've found a weally big fox.'

'Didn't you hear a sort of *Wooooo* noise?' asked Bunty doubtfully. 'Foxes don't make that sort of noise, do they?'

'Oh, the typical Bwitish fox makes hundweds of diffewent sounds,' said Cousin Kenneth. 'You can twust an expert like me to know when the hounds wun acwoss a fox. Come along, let's huwwy after them.'

In the clearing Hamish was still swinging from his branch, crying 'Woooooooo!'. Then the branch broke.

'Oh, my baby!' cried Pam, running forward. But at that moment one of the Barty Hounds bounded into the clearing. 'Woof!' it barked, seeing the fur-clad figure rolling on the ground. 'Woof! Woof!' Another dog followed, and then another.

Hamish took one look, got to his feet, and ran.

'They've definitely found the fox, Melanie,'

called Thomas from his bike. 'Come on, let's go and see.'

'I think it's horrible,' answered Melanie, but she followed Thomas into the wood.

Certainly the hounds were in full pursuit of something. It ran a little way ahead of them, puffing and panting, and when they began to snap at its heels it climbed up a tree. The dogs stood at the bottom of the trunk, baying.

'Where is it? Where is it?' called Cousin Kenneth, riding up with Bunty just behind him.

'It's gone up the tree, Mr Honourable,' answered Mr Majeika, who had managed to catch up with the hounds.

'Nonsense,' snapped Bunty Brace-Girdle. 'Foxes don't climb trees, you silly little man.'

'Well, Bunty, this one has,' said Mr Potter, and at that moment the branch broke and the furry creature came tumbling to the ground.

'Good grief!' cried Bunty Brace-Girdle. 'Run for your lives! It's not a fox, it's a gorilla!'

'A gowilla!' yelled Cousin Kenneth, terrified.
'A gowilla! A gowilla!'

'Don't worry, Mrs Brace-Girdle,' said
Thomas, riding his bike into the clearing. 'It's
only Hamish Bigmore.' He pulled back the top
of the gorilla suit to reveal a very out-of-breath
Hamish.

'My baby!' screamed Pam Bigmore, running
forward. 'How dare you chase my baby with
your cruel doggies? I'll have the Society for
Cruelty to Children on to you all.'

'Excuse me,' said Mr Potter, interrupting the
uproar, 'but I've just seen a fox walk by.'

Twenty minutes later, the Hunt was a mile or two away, chasing the fox across open country, and Mr Majeika was sitting on the steps of the windmill with his head in his hands. His horse was grazing quietly in a nearby field. Thomas and Melanie were sitting with him.

'So you don't like hunting, Mr Majeika?' asked Melanie.

Mr Majeika shook his head. 'I thought chasing the fox was bad enough, Melanie, but Mr Potter didn't tell me that when they've caught it, they're going to *kill* it. A tear began to trickle down his cheek.

'Well, Mr Majeika,' said Thomas, 'what would you do with the fox if you caught it? Tuck it up in bed and give it a nice hot drink?'

Mr Majeika thought for a moment. 'Yes, Thomas,' he said, 'that's exactly what I'd do. In fact, it's what I'm going to do now.'

Melanie stared. 'But how are you going to

find it, Mr Majeika?' she asked. 'It's at least a mile away. Are you going to run after it?'

'No, Melanie,' answered Mr Majeika. 'I'm going to give a Walpurgian whistle.'

Before Thomas and Melanie could ask what he meant, he had flicked his tuft of hair — a sign that he was about to do some magic — and stuck two fingers in his mouth. Then he whistled.

Thomas and Melanie couldn't hear the whistle, but they could feel it. It made them shiver all over. The trees and grass around them seemed to shiver too, and for a moment the birds stopped singing. Then everything was back to normal again.

On the other side of the wood, where the Hunt had gathered, Mr Potter was looking puzzled. 'The fox seems to have disappeared,' he said. 'The hounds were right on top of it a moment ago, but I swear I saw it streak through the trees, and there's no sign of it now.'

The hounds were sniffing round in a puzzled fashion; they seemed to have lost the scent.

'Wubbish,' said Cousin Kenneth bossily. 'An expewienced huntsman like me will vewy soon find it. Huwwy up, and we'll wecapture the scent.'

'Here it comes!' whispered Melanie, and there was a rustle at the edge of the woodland by the windmill as something small and brown trotted out.

When it saw the three of them, the fox stopped nervously. Mr Majeika got to his feet and walked towards it slowly in a funny waddling

fashion ('That's a Walpurgian Walk,' whispered
Thomas to Melanie). When he was near the fox,
he got to his knees and waited for the fox to
come cautiously forward, until it was in front of
him. Then the two of them rubbed noses ('A
Walpurgian greeting,' whispered Thomas).

Next Mr Majeika made a series of barking
noises, like a dog with a sore throat. The fox
answered back in the same fashion. The two of
them were evidently having a conversation.

After a few minutes of this, Mr Majeika got
to his feet and came towards Thomas and

Melanie. The fox trotted away into the woodland.

'Won't it come with us?' asked Melanie.

'Oh yes,' said Mr Majeika. 'It's very grateful to be offered a hiding place from those horrid hounds. But it wants to go and fetch its wife and children.'

Half an hour later, the Much Barty Hunt was wandering gloomily through the wood. They had seen no further sign of the fox, and everyone was cross and tired. 'What's more,' said Mr Potter gloomily, 'I think there's going to be a thunderstorm.'

The storm was Mr Majeika's idea. He had asked Walpurgis to send one, because he thought it would drive the Hunt People home, so that there was no chance they would see the fox bringing its family to safety in the windmill. Up in Walpurgis, the Worshipful Wizard had decided to do Mr Majeika proud, and he arranged for the mightiest of storms to break over Much Barty.

There were great flashes of lightning and crashes of thunder, and down came the rain. In a moment the Hunt were all drenched. Water was running off the hounds' backs, and Bunty Brace-Girdle's hair was streaming in her eyes. Even Cousin Kenneth was looking sorry for himself: his antique top hat, which had belonged to the famous John Peel, had gone all soggy.

So they set off home; but the rain came down worse than ever, and about half a mile outside Much Barty, Bunty Brace-Girdle had an idea. 'I say! That fellow Majeika's windmill is just across that field. Why don't we go and shelter there, until the rain stops?'

'I'm not surprised they were cross,' said Thomas. 'But to give you the sack . . . !'

'Just because you spoiled their horrid hunting,' said Melanie.

'I'll never forget their faces,' said Mr Majeika, 'when they came through the door, and found the fox curled up in a basket in front of the fire, with its wife and children.'

'Mummy went so red in the face I thought she was going to burst,' said Melanie.

'And your Cousin Kenneth almost fainted, he was so angry,' said Thomas. 'Oh, how funny it was!'

'And then they tried to grab the fox,' said

Melanie, 'and you wiggled your tuft of hair, Mr Majeika, and the fire began to pour out clouds of smoke – you'd magicked it – so that they couldn't see a thing. And when the smoke cleared, the fox and his family had run away.'

'It was brilliant,' said Thomas. 'The cleverest thing you've done, Mr Majeika.'

'Yes, it was,' said Mr Majeika gloomily. 'But it got me the sack.'

'I'm sure Mr Potter didn't really want to sack you from the school,' said Melanie. 'He likes you really. But Mummy's a school governor, and she was so furious that he had to do something.'

'And I thought nothing could be worse than not having you as our teacher,' said Thomas.

'But there is something worse,' said Melanie. 'Do you know who Mummy has persuaded Mr Potter to take on in your place? Cousin Kenneth!'

A few hours later, Thomas and Melanie were helping Mr Majeika move his things out of the

windmill, while Bunty and Cousin Kenneth
bustled in with some new furniture. 'It isn't fair,
Mummy,' protested Melanie. 'Mr Majeika
found the windmill for himself, and made it a
comfy place to live, when he first came to
Much Barty. It's *his* home, and no one else's.'

'The silly little man hasn't got any documents
to prove he owns it, have you, Mr Majeika?'
snapped Bunty. Mr Majeika shook his head
miserably. 'In that case,' continued Bunty, we
may assume it goes with the job.'

'So where are you going to live now, Mr Majeika?' asked Thomas.

'There's only one place that will take me in,' said Mr Majeika sadly. 'The Home for Distressed Teachers.'

'By the way, Majeika, or whatever your name is,' snorted Cousin Kenneth, as he carried a stuffed fox in a glass case into the windmill, 'Cousin Bunty tells me I may have a bit of twouble with one of your pupils, a chap named Hamish Bigmore. Have you got any advice about how to stop him being unwuly?'

'Well,' said Mr Majeika thoughtfully, 'I know what *I* did, the first time Hamish caused trouble.'

'Oh?' said Cousin Kenneth. 'What was that? Did you give him detention, or six of the best with a wuler?'

'No,' said Mr Majeika. 'I turned him into a fwog.'

Much to his surprise, Mr Majeika found that life in the Home for Distressed Teachers was very nice indeed. The food was good, he was allowed to stay in bed in the morning as long as he liked (he had taken his hammock with him from the windmill), and there was a friend to keep him company – Miss Flavia Jelly, who had taught at the school before Mr Majeika came down to Britland. She had been driven into retirement, in the Home for Distressed Teachers, by the awful behaviour of Hamish Bigmore.

Mr Majeika and Miss Jelly spent many pleasant hours together – not least because Mr Majeika found that the Home for Distressed Teachers allowed people who lived there to keep pets. The two of them spent hours feeding and stroking and playing with Mr Majeika's pets, which he kept in his room.

'I'd never have guessed they were such sweet little creatures, Mr Majeika,' said Miss Jelly.

'Yes, indeed,' said Mr Majeika. 'They're perfectly lovely.'

It was only a week later when he was riding his tricycle past the school that he saw the ambulance. Cousin Kenneth was being carried out to it on a stretcher, and he no longer looked red in the face. He was deathly pale, and seemed to be gibbering to himself. Mr Potter was following the ambulance-men, anxiously rubbing his hands.

'Ah, Majeika,' he said. 'The usual trouble, I'm afraid.'

'Hamish Bigmore, Mr Potter?' asked Mr Majeika.

'Exactly so, Majeika. Our Hamish has been a little too much for Cousin Kenneth.' Indeed, Mr Majeika could see Hamish grinning wickedly from the classroom window.

The ambulance drove Cousin Kenneth off to hospital. Mr Potter watched it go, then cleared his throat. 'I don't know quite how to put this Majeika but, er, would you like your old job back?'

Bunty Brace-Girdle came out of the school entrance. 'Yes, Mr Majeika,' she said. 'We have to admit that you have, well, a certain touch with Hamish Bigmore that no one else can equal. Would you be willing to come back and teach again?'

'Oh, please do, Mr Majeika,' said Thomas and Melanie, who had run out of the school too. 'We do so want you back.'

'Very well,' said Mr Majeika, 'but on one condition. I must be allowed to bring my pets with me.'

'Your pets, Majeika?' asked Mr Potter.

'That's right,' said Mr Majeika. 'Ah, here they come now. Miss Jelly is just taking them for an afternoon walk.' And round the corner came Flavia Jelly, leading the fox and his family, who were trotting merrily after her.

Bunty Brace-Girdle went red in the face. 'But – but –' she spluttered, 'this is preposterous! What about the Much Barty Hunt?'

Mr Majeika smiled. 'The Much Barty Hunt, Mrs Brace-Girdle,' he said, 'will not be meeting again. At least, not while I'm teaching in Much Barty. Is that correct, Mr Potter?'

Mr Potter drew a deep breath. 'Yes, Majeika,' he sighed. 'It's absolutely correct. Now, perhaps you'd like to take your pets to the school kitchen, and give them a nice meal?'

'Thank you, Mr Potter,' said Mr Majeika. 'I shall be delighted — and so will they!'

The Walpurgian giggle book

This is the book from which all the Christmas cracker jokes come. They are almost as old as the wizard who collects them.

Dad: I was working as a Father Christmas but they gave me the sack.
Kid: So why are you smiling?
Dad: It was full of toys!

Witch: Quick! Quick! Fetch my broomstick!
Wizard: Do you want to fly off on a journey?
Witch: No, I've spilt a packet of Corn Flakes and I want to sweep it up.

'Knock, knock!'
   'Who's there?'
'Witch.'
   'Witch who?'
'Which of you is going to open the door and let me in?'

Wizard: Little boy, if you don't behave yourself, I'm going to turn you into the ugliest person in the world.

Boy: I see you've been practising on my dad.

Witch: Waiter, there's a toad in my soup.

Waiter: So sorry, Madam. I forgot that you prefer them on toast.

Why did the witches go to Liverpool?

For a Witch-Dock-Tour (witch doctor).

'Good morning. I'm the Invisible Man.'

'Yes, I see you are.'

Mother ghost to cheeky toddler ghost: 'Don't spook until you're spooken to.'

What do you call cleaners in a haunted house?

Ghostdusters.

First Ghost: What did you see at the theatre?

Second Ghost: A phantomime.

Wizard: Here's a piece of paper that will make you fly very high in the sky.

Girl: What sort of spell is it?

Wizard: It isn't a spell, it's a ticket to New York.

Witch: Waiter, waiter, I don't like the taste of this dog-biscuit.

Waiter: But I made it myself, madam, with fresh dog.

First Ghost: I don't like watching horror films.

Second Ghost: Why not?

First Ghost: They nearly frighten the life into me.

What do you get if you cross a witch with an ice cube?

A cold spell.

What disease does a witch get from flying too near a galaxy?

Star warts.

Have yourself a wizard little Christmas

Upstairs in Walpurgis they were having a peaceful time. The Worshipful Wizard had just announced the beginning of the annual Wizards' Hibernation. 'I advise you,' he told them all, via the Wizards' Radio (Walpurgian World Service), 'to set your alarm clocks to ring when wildest winter gives way to sunny spring.' The prospect of a good three months' sleep was making him quite poetical.

Downstairs in Britland it was anything but peaceful. Mr Potter, the headmaster of St Barty's School, was trying to organize the Christmas decorations, and there were paper chains all over the place, and holly lying about just where you were likely to sit on it. 'If only Mr Majeika were here to help,' sighed Mr

Potter desperately. 'I can't think what's keeping him.'

Neither could Thomas or Melanie, so they set off for Mr Majeika's windmill to see what had happened to him. On the door was a notice: 'HIBERNATION IN PROGRESS. DO NOT DISTURB.'

'Oh no!' said Thomas. 'That means he's not waking up till spring!'

They opened the door, and sure enough,

there was Mr Majeika, snoring in his hammock. What was worse, nothing would wake him – they tried shaking him, shouting, and tickling. Then Thomas saw the Spell Book open on the table, and after studying it he managed to find a spell for waking Slumbering Wizards by pricking them with Christmas holly. So a few minutes later, he and Melanie were back with some holly, which did the trick, though they had to apply several doses before Mr Majeika was wide awake enough to pedal his tricycle to school.

By the time he got there, Mr Potter was looking anxiously at his watch. 'Ah, there you are at last, Majeika,' he said. 'All ready, I hope, for the most exciting day of the school year – the day we break up for Christmas. Now, will you please go and bring in the tree.'

'Tree, Mr Potter?' asked Mr Majeika vaguely, looking out of the window at the enormous oak trees in the school garden. 'You want me to fetch a tree?' He felt it would require all his magical powers to bring one of the oaks indoors.

'The *Christmas* tree, Majeika,' snapped Mr Potter. 'It's just outside the back door. Do hurry! There's an awful lot still to be done.'

Mr Majeika went and fetched the tree. He ran into Mrs Brace-Girdle, Melanie's mother, who was carrying a bucket decorated with red crepe paper. 'Ah, Mr Majeika,' she said briskly, 'here's the bucket for the tree.' Mr Majeika took the bucket, propped the tree up against a

chair, and tried to hang the bucket from one of the branches. 'No, no,' snapped Bunty Brace-Girdle, 'the tree *stands* in the bucket!'

Mr Majeika sighed and did as he was told. Really, he would never make head or tail of these Britlanders. So this was how they celebrated their famous Christmas, about which he had heard so much. They took a strange kind of tree and stood it in a bucket. He sighed again, and wished he had been allowed to hibernate in peace.

*

At the North Pole, someone else was in the same state of mind. Santa Claus's alarm clock had just rung, and he couldn't believe what time it was. 'Oh no!' he groaned. 'Not Christmas already!'

He threw his alarm clock across the bedroom, and turned over to go to sleep again. But a voice broke in on his doze. 'And a very merry Christmas to you, sir!' It was Rudolph, the chief reindeer, and the alarm clock was hanging from one of his antlers, where it had just landed.

'Merry Christmas, Rudolph,' grunted Santa. He felt anything but merry. Looking out of the window, he could see how cold it was. Why did he have to make his journey with all those millions of toys at the coldest time of the year? It wasn't fair!

'And now, sir,' said Rudolph, 'prepare yourself for some bad news. We have a crisis on our hands.'

'A crisis?' said Santa nervously.

'The reindeer have all been taken ill, sir. An outbreak of Hoofamatosis.'

'Hoofamatosis?' said Santa suspiciously. 'Just as Christmas is coming? More likely Lazyitis if you ask me.'

Crossly, he pulled on his boots and strode out to the stables. 'Now listen here!' he announced to Rudolph's fellow reindeer, as they lay groaning in their stalls. 'At the latest estimate we have thirty-eight million toys to deliver, across the entire planet Earth, and only one night of the year in which to do it.'

In reply, the reindeer groaned. 'Couldn't you call out a vet, sir?' suggested Rudolph.

'Have you forgotten,' stormed Santa, 'that Vetinerary Pox, the wizard animal-surgeon, is asleep in Walpurgis for the winter? Now listen here, you lazy lot. Do you think *I* like struggling out of my cosy bunk each midwinter, exposing my tender bits to the freezing air, and then squeezing my precious tum into someone's narrow, filthy chimney, not to mention getting my beautiful face sooty, and having to balance on all those rooftops —'

Santa stopped in mid-sentence. Panic had struck him. Every Christmas was a nightmare to him because *he was terrified of heights!*

Meanwhile, at St Barty's School, they were rehearsing the Nativity Play. This year the play was being organized by Mr Majeika's worst pupil, Hamish Bigmore. Mr Potter had been pleasantly surprised when Hamish had offered to do it – it was so unlike Hamish's usual unhelpful behaviour – but now Mr Potter could see why he had asked to be in charge.

'S'me, Hamish Bigmore!' he was announcing to the cast. 'I'm the Director, Producer, Writer, Scenic Designer, Costume Designer, Front of House Manager, and of course the star of this year's Nativity Play.'

'Which will, I'm sure,' muttered Mr Potter gloomily, 'be topped in enjoyment only by Mrs Fudd's Christmas lunch.'

Mrs Fudd was the school cook. Her specialities were soggy mashed potato, burnt sausages, and undercooked rice pudding. At the moment, she was trying to follow what the recipe book said for Christmas lunch. 'Roast the turkey, make the gravy, take the lumps out of the gravy, make the pudding.' She smiled as she read this last instruction. 'I'm famous for my puddings,' she said to herself.

She was indeed. Mr Potter had said to her, 'Mrs Fudd, I will never, as long as I live, forget your puddings,' and this was perfectly true. The last one she had made tasted like india-rubber, and when Mr Potter had tried to flush it down the loo, it wouldn't go.

Mrs Fudd went round the school kitchen, taking ingredients and putting them in the mixing bowl. 'Caster sugar,' she read from her recipe book, and poured out from a packet which she thought said *Caster Sugar* on it. But she had left her glasses on the table; what the packet really said was *Cat Litter*.

'Stir in one egg,' read Mrs Fudd from the book. She felt about on the table for an egg, and picked up something that felt like one. She cracked it on the side of the bowl, and stirred it in.

It was her glasses.

*

Back at the North Pole, Santa was in a misery. All the reindeer except Rudolph had refused to go; they said they were far too ill. Rudolph insisted that he could manage by himself, but Santa, who was already terrified of flying, became even more nervous as he thought of making the journey with just one reindeer.

'It's no good,' he muttered. 'We're bound to crash.'

Rudolph sighed, remembering what an awful time they had had last year. First of all, Santa had forgotten half the toys (about twenty million of them), and they had to turn round and go back for them to the North Pole. Then, when they reached Britland, he had insisted on drinking all the glasses of sherry that had been left out for him, to steady his nerves, with the result that he had kept falling down chimneys. It had been perfectly awful.

'May I suggest, sir,' said Rudolph, as he watched Santa bumbling around, trying to load the sleigh with toys, while also attempting to fill his hot-water-bottle and look for his muffler and mittens (which of course had gone missing, just as they did every Christmas), 'may I

suggest, most respectfully, that you buck up and get your act together . . . *sir*?' Really, he thought to himself, Santa was quite hopeless at the job. It was high time they gave him a year off, and let someone else have a go.

*

'And this year's Nativity Play,' announced Mr Potter to the audience of parents, 'is completely the work of Hamish Bigmore . . . ' (there was some applause, mostly from Hamish's mother, Pam Bigmore, who occupied a seat in the middle of the front row)' . . . who also stars as the Innkeeper.' Mr Potter walked off stage as Hamish came on. 'I don't remember the Innkeeper playing that big a part, do you, Majeika?' muttered Mr Potter.

'Oh, it's all new to me, Mr Potter,' said Mr Majeika, wondering what the play would be about.

At that moment, Mrs Fudd came into the school hall, wiping her hands on her apron and looking anxious. 'Mr Potter,' she said glumly, 'that there school oven has packed up. I always said it'd break down sooner or later and now it has. And I can't cook the Christmas turkey!'

Mr Potter looked wretched. 'Oh dear, oh dear,' he said. 'Whatever are we going to do? The most important day of the school year, and it'll be ruined.'

Mr Majeika thought for a moment. 'Leave it to me, Mr Potter,' he said briskly, and bustled off to the kitchen.

'Where's Mr Majeika?' hissed Hamish Bigmore from the stage. 'I need him as the Storyteller.' He thrust the script of the Nativity Play at Mr Potter.

Mr Potter looked around him, then passed the script to Mrs Fudd. 'Just the person,' he said to her. 'Your stage debut, Mrs Fudd.'

Mrs Fudd looked very surprised to be drawn into the proceedings, but she went on to the stage and began to read from Hamish's script.

'And it came to pass that Mary and Joseph had to go to Bethlehem to be taxed. And because they was so poor, they went by monkey.'

'Donkey,' hissed Hamish Bigmore.

'And they put up at an old inn,' continued Mrs Fudd, 'what was run by a delightful innkeeper — what's wearing my tea-towel!' snapped Mrs Fudd, pulling off Hamish Bigmore's home-made head-dress.

In the school kitchen, Mr Majeika was trying to make head or tail of Mrs Fudd's messy preparations for the meal. There were bowls, saucepans, and dishes full of mysterious mixtures, which all looked quite disgusting — very far from the delicious meal of Mugwort Morsels and Bat's Blood soup with which Walpurgians, before they began to hibernate, always celebrated the Winter Solstice (see recipes on p. 124–127).

'Still,' thought Mr Majeika, 'I reckon I know the kind of thing Thomas and Melanie would enjoy.' He flicked the tuft of hair which stood up in the centre of his head – a sure sign that magic was on the way – and there was a flash and a puff of smoke. Suddenly, out of nowhere, a delicious Christmas cake stood in the middle of the kitchen table.

That would do fine for teatime, but there was still the problem of lunch to sort out. Mr Majeika saw that Mrs Fudd's Christmas pudding was boiling away merrily on the stove, but the oven remained unlit and the turkey unroasted. The only thing to do was, once again, some magic.

He popped the turkey into the oven, shut the door, and flicked his tuft. It was supposed to be a spell to make the oven very hot very quickly; but Mr Majeika had failed his Sorcery Exams, in Walpurgis, time and again (which was why he was down here in Britland as a teacher), and as so often happened with him, the spell went wrong.

There was a frightful explosion, and when

the smoke had cleared, all Mr Majeika's hair had vanished from his head – except the tuft in the middle! He looked terrible!

Worse still, when he opened the oven and peered inside, he saw that the turkey was burnt to a cinder!

What on earth was he going to do? Desperately, he tried flicking the tuft – yes, it still worked – and muttering another spell. Again, there was an explosion, and Mr Majeika shut his eyes, not daring for a long while to look at what had happened.

When at last he opened them, there was a lovely Christmas dinner set out on the table.

'Crikey!' gasped Mrs Fudd, who had deserted the Nativity Play and rushed into the kitchen to see what all the noise was about, 'you've done a bloomin' marvellous job, Mr Majeika!'

The lunch went down extremely well when it was served, especially the pudding. (Mr Majeika's magic had got rid of the Cat Litter.)

'Look,' said Thomas, delving with his spoon into his dish. 'I've got a silver sixpence!'

'And I've got one too!' said Melanie.

In fact everyone had one except Hamish Bigmore. When he prodded his pudding to see if anything special was hidden in it, he soon found something hard, but it wasn't a sixpence. 'Yuck!' he spluttered. 'It's a pair of glasses!'

'Well, well,' said Mr Majeika, munching his way happily through the meal, 'I am enjoying Christmas, Mr Potter. Such a delicious meal. Quite delicious,' he continued, picking a piece of holly off his pudding, and starting to chew it. 'Quite, quite delicious.'

At the North Pole, Santa had just finished loading up the sleigh. 'Let's get it over with,' he muttered to Rudolph.

'I hate to mention it, sir,' said Rudolph, 'but aren't we a tiny bit early? Christmas Eve doesn't start for another twelve hours.'

'I know, Rudolph,' muttered Santa, 'but I want to allow plenty of time for the journey. Let's go as slowly as possible, then I might find the flying a bit less frightening.'

'Flying, sir?' said Rudolph. 'You don't mean to say you're frightened of *that* as well? I know you hate the rooftops, and the chimneys, sir, but I thought you didn't mind flying in the sleigh.'

'I'm afraid my nerve has gone, Rudolph,' said Santa miserably. 'The whole thing just terrifies me from start to finish. Come along, let's get it over with.' He climbed in to the sleigh and gave the reins a twitch. Rudolph took the strain, and a moment later the sleigh was rising far above the North Pole, into the sky.

'All right back there, sir?' called Rudolph as they levelled out at thirty thousand feet.

'No, Rudolph,' answered Santa miserably. 'I'm bloomin' well not all right. My Flying Potion fell off the sleigh just as we took off, and without it I'll be an absolute nervous wreck. Aaaaaarrghhh!' he cried, as the sleigh hit a current of air, and began to sway up and down like a big dipper. 'I can't stand it! I'm going to shut my eyes, Rudolph, and keep them shut until we get there.'

'I shouldn't do that, sir,' called Rudolph. 'After all, someone has to read the map.'

But it was too late. Santa had pulled a rug over his head, and wouldn't answer.

'Oh dear,' sighed Rudolph to himself. 'Somehow I think it's going to be one of those Christmases.'

*

A few hours later, on the morning of Christmas Eve, Mr Majeika was sweeping his front steps at the windmill when Thomas and Melanie came hurrying up the path. 'Mr

Majeika!' they called, 'Mr Majeika!'

Mr Majeika greeted them. 'What's that you're carrying?' he asked them.

'It's our Christmas present to you,' Melanie explained. 'You mustn't open it till tomorrow.'

'Christmas present?' echoed Mr Majeika, his face falling.

'What's the matter, Mr Majeika?' said Thomas, worried. 'Don't you want to have a present from us?'

'Of course I do, Thomas,' answered Mr Majeika. 'It's just that, where I come from, if someone gives you a present, you must give them one back. And I haven't got one for you!'

'Don't worry, Mr Majeika,' said Melanie. 'You've got till tomorrow. I'm sure you can think of something.'

'And by the way,' said Thomas, 'don't forget that tonight is the Village Carol Singing.'

'Carol Singing?' echoed Mr Majeika. 'What in the name of Walpurgis is that?'

'It's when grown-ups traipse around pretending to be jolly, instead of grumpy as usual,' said Melanie.

'But what do they sing?' asked Mr Majeika.

'Oh,' said Thomas, 'stuff like "Oh Come All Ye Frightful."'

'And don't forget to hang up your stocking, will you, Mr Majeika?' said Melanie.

'My stocking?' echoed Mr Majeika.

'That's right,' said Thomas. 'Do you know what you'll find in it on Christmas morning?'

'I've no idea,' said Mr Majeika. 'A foot?'

Rudolph was right. It was definitely turning out to be one of those Christmases. The sleigh had nearly crashed into the Atlantic, and now they were approaching Britland at about five thousand miles an hour. Rudolph tried to slow down, but the winds were very strong behind them, and Santa was still hiding under the rug and refusing to look.

'Can't you do something, sir?' he called.
'We're supposed to start delivering presents in
the north of Scotland, but right now we're
heading for Brighton.'

Santa gave a feeble twitch on the reins, but
it was no use. Out of control, the sleigh
careered down from the sky, towards . . . Much
Barty.

In the windmill, Mr Majeika was dozing by
the fire, trying to think of a present for Thomas
and Melanie. He nodded off to sleep . . . and
dreamt that something enormous was crashing
into the windmill.

He woke up to find that it was.

93

There was a terrible rending sound as something heavy struck one of the sails, then a thump and a tearing of wood. Most of the ceiling fell down on Mr Majeika, leaving a gaping hole.

Mr Majeika gasped and blinked, and then ran outside, fearing that the rest of the windmill was about to crash down on top of him.

'Help!' called a voice. 'Help! I'm stuck up here!' Clinging to one of the sails of the windmill was a fat man with a white beard, dressed in a red jacket, trousers, and heavy boots. 'Help!' he was calling. 'Help! Help!'

Mr Majeika stared at him. There was something familiar about the fellow. 'Is your name by any chance Nick?' he called.

'That's right,' called the person in the beard. 'Nick Christmas, alias Santa Claus. Now for goodness' sake please help me down.'

'Nick Christmas!' said Mr Majeika in astonishment. 'Well, well. I thought I recognized you. Don't you remember? We were at school together.'

At six o'clock the Carol Singing party assembled at Mrs Bunty Brace-Girdle's house. 'Majeika's late again,' said Mr Potter, looking at his watch.

'Mr Majeika?' said Bunty. 'Surely we don't want *him* in our party, Mr Potter?'

'Oh, but Bunty,' explained Mr Potter, 'he'll be ever so useful — he's such a good-natured chap that I'm sure he'll eat Miss Haddock's mince pies. And you know no one else will.'

'So that's where you've been all these years,' Mr Majeika was saying to Santa Claus, who was lying on Mr Majeika's bed, still looking very shaky. 'At the North Pole?'

'Yes,' groaned Santa, rubbing his bruises. 'Two hundred and ninety-nine years, to be precise. It's a steady enough little number for most of the year – just making toys quietly by myself. But then comes this awful journey!' He groaned again.

'Poor old Nick,' said Mr Majeika.

Some more of the ceiling fell down, and a face looked through at them. It was Rudolph. 'And what about poor old me?' he enquired. 'Did anybody by any chance remember that there's a stone cold reindeer who's been stuck out on the top of this bloomin' windmill for the last half hour? *Sir?*'

They had just managed to get Rudolph down when Thomas and Melanie could be heard approaching the windmill. 'Mr Majeika!' they were calling. 'Mr Majeika!'

Santa Claus turned white behind his beard. 'Smalls!' he cried. 'They mustn't set eyes on me in this condition!'

Rudolph quickly took charge of the situation. 'Upstairs, sir, and quick!' he told Santa.

Mr Majeika went to the front door just as

Thomas and Melanie were coming up the steps. 'Children!' he said nervously. 'What on earth are you doing here?'

'You've forgotten all about Mummy's Carol Singing party, haven't you, Mr Majeika?' said Melanie.

'You're late, very late', said Thomas.

Mr Majeika felt thoroughly flustered. 'I'm afraid I can't come out now,' he said anxiously. 'I've got . . . visitors.'

'Visitors?' echoed Melanie suspiciously.

'Not someone from Walpurgis, is it?' asked Thomas.

Mr Majeika shook his head. 'Certainly not. If you really want to know, they're from the North Pole. Now, I really must go and look after them.' He started to go into the windmill.

Melanie's eyes widened. 'The North Pole?' she asked.

'Not — ?' said Thomas. And then he saw a pair of snow-covered boots standing just inside the door. 'You mean, Mr Majeika, you're really having a visit from Santa Claus?'

Mr Majeika tried to keep up the pretence that there was no one special in the windmill, but Thomas and Melanie wouldn't be put off, and eventually they persuaded him to let them tiptoe upstairs and peep round the door at Santa. 'He's probably asleep,' whispered Mr Majeika, 'so it won't do any harm.'

But Santa was wide awake, and he turned pale when he saw their faces coming round the door. 'Oh no!' he gasped. 'I've been Seen! Now I'm bound to lose my job.'

'Why aren't you out delivering presents?' asked Melanie.

'Santa had a little accident,' said a voice behind them. It was Rudolph, peering out of the wardrobe where Mr Majeika had tried to hide him.

'Gosh!' said Thomas. 'Are you really Rudolph the Red Nosed Reindeer?'

'Well, I'm not Puss in Boots,' said Rudolph.

'Did you fail your Sorcery Exams too?'
Melanie asked Santa.

'No,' laughed Rudolph. 'His driving test!'

'But Mr Majeika, what am I going to do?'
moaned Santa. 'My sleigh is broken to pieces.
And if I don't deliver all those toys to all the
Smalls tonight, they'll stop believing in me.'

'He's right,' said Thomas. 'You've got to do
something, Mr Majeika.'

'Leave it to me!' said Mr Majeika. He was
frightfully pleased that everyone was turning

to him to save the situation. On the other hand, he hadn't the faintest idea what to do.

Up in Walpurgis, the wizards were snoring happily. Hibernation had begun.

Suddenly, a distant cry disturbed their slumber. 'Sir! Sir! Majeika calling! Worshipful Wizard, sir! Majeika calling! Help needed!'

The Worshipful Wizard stirred crossly. 'Problems, Majeika?' he asked without opening his eyes. Really, that little fellow down in

Britland was a perpetual pest. It might have been better to have kept him in Walpurgis, rather than to have sent him away just because he kept failing his Sorcery Exams.

'Just one problem, sir,' answered Mr Majeika's voice. 'It's Santa Claus, sir. He's crash-landed in Britland, sir, and he can't continue with his rounds. He's asked *me* to save the situation, sir.'

'Quite right, Majeika,' said the Worshipful Wizard, yawning. 'Quite right. That's the best answer.'

'What is, sir?' asked Mr Majeika, puzzled.

'What you said, Majeika. *You* save the situation. Do the job yourself. Take over as Santa Claus.'

'What, sir? Me, sir?' cried Mr Majeika, feeling faint. 'Oh, no, sir, not that. Please, sir, do try and think of something else!'

But it was too late. The Worshipful Wizard had gone back to sleep and this time, try as Mr Majeika could, nothing would waken him.

'Don't worry,' said Melanie, when Mr Majeika told her the news. 'We'll help you.'

But where on earth am I going to get a Santa Claus outfit in a hurry?' asked Mr Majeika desperately. 'Santa won't let me wear his own clothes. He says he'll freeze in just his underwear. And anyway, they wouldn't fit me — he's far too fat.'

'*I* know,' said Thomas excitedly. 'There's a Santa costume at Melanie's house. Her mother was going to get you to wear it, Mr Majeika, when you went round with the collecting box for the Carol Singers. It'll do nicely!'

Melanie ran down to her house, took the costume without anyone noticing, and smuggled it back to the windmill. By this time, Thomas had managed to rig up Mr Majeika's tricycle so that it looked a bit like Santa's sleigh.

'Well done, both of you,' said Mr Majeika. 'I've tried to persuade Santa to do the job instead of me, but he absolutely refuses — says his nerves are all in pieces, and he couldn't possibly do it without his Flying Potion, which fell off the sleigh at the North Pole. And Rudolph absolutely refuses to come too, so I haven't got a reindeer.'

'Leave it to us!' said Thomas and Melanie, and they hurried off to the village pub, the Barty Arms, returning a few minutes later with a stag's head which they had borrowed from the wall of the Saloon Bar.

'Well,' said Rudolph bitterly to Santa Claus as they looked out of the windmill at the preparations going on below, 'I hope you're satisfied, sir, that this year the legendary partnership of Santa and Rudolph is being replaced by a Failed Wizard and a stag's head from a pub.'

'You will remember the Red Claus Code, won't you, Majeika?' called Santa anxiously. 'Go as quietly as possible, never be seen by anyone, and leave a present for every Small — no matter how horrible.'

'Twenty-eight . . . twenty-nine . . . ' counted Hamish Bigmore, as he went around his house, hanging up stockings and pillowcases. Last year his parents had given him three hundred and sixty-five toys for Christmas, and this year he knew there would be even more.

'Are you sure you've hung up enough, Hamie dear?' called his mother, Mrs Pam Bigmore, thinking of all the parcels from expensive London shops that she had waiting for Hamish, stacked up in the garage. 'Do make sure there's enough room for all the presents Santa's going to bring.'

'Don't talk rubbish,' sneered Hamish. 'There's no such person as Santa Claus.'

'Really?' answered his mother vaguely. 'I always thought there was.' She watched proudly as Hamish went on counting his stockings and pillowcases.

'Thirty . . . thirty-one . . . thirty-two . . . '

*

'All right,' whispered Mr Majeika to Thomas and Melanie. 'Give me a push, and off I go.'

They were on the edge of the village, and Mr Majeika's tricycle was laden with presents from Santa's broken sleigh. There was only room for about a hundred or so, just enough for the children of Much Barty, and Mr Majeika couldn't think for the life of him how he was going to cope with the millions of others, or the journey across the world. But he had to make a start somewhere.

'Of course,' said Rudolph, looking gloomily out of the windmill at the darkening sky, 'he's never going to make it, sir, never in a month of Christmases.'

If Thomas and Melanie had overheard this, they would have been inclined to agree.

Down in the village, the Carol Singing party had set out on its rounds. Thomas and Melanie joined it at the village pond. It would give them a chance to keep an eye on Mr Majeika, who, if he kept to schedule, ought to be slipping down the nearby chimneys in a few minutes.

'And where have you two been?' asked Melanie's mother when she saw them.

'Helping Santa Claus, Mummy,' said Melanie, who saw no reason not to tell the truth.

'Don't be silly, Melanie,' said Bunty Brace-Girdle. 'Now, come along and take these collecting boxes.'

'Ding Dong! Merrily on high,' sang the Carol Singers, under Mr Potter's direction, *'In Heaven the bells are ringing.'*

'Ding Dong! There he goes now!' sang Thomas and Melanie, pointing at Mr Majeika, whom they could just see scrambling about on a roof top at the edge of the village green. *'I hope he knows what he's doing!'*

Mr Majeika did not know what he was doing – not at all. He had already fallen off three rooftops, got stuck in five chimneys, knocked over a Christmas tree, and broken a window. At one house he was nearly eaten alive by a savage dog; at another, he was lucky to escape with his life when he slid down a chimney and found himself sitting inside a kitchen stove. It had taken all the magic powers he possessed to rescue himself, and he was getting exhausted. If he didn't stop for a breather soon, he knew he'd break a leg, or worse.

Another thing about the job was that no one had bothered to leave him a nice letter, or a thank-you note. The children had all hung up their stockings without so much as a piece of paper saying 'Please', and Mr Majeika began to wonder why Santa made all this effort every year, considering that no one seemed to appreciate him. Only at one house was it different.

This was School Cottage, where Mr Potter lived, and the headmaster had left a charming letter pinned to his stocking:

Dear Santa,
    Dudley Cicero Potter here again, Santa. I have written to you for the past fifty years for a train set. I have not yet received a train set, Santa, but maybe this year I'll be lucky, eh?
                        Yours hopefully,
                        Dudley Potter.

Mr Majeika searched in his sack of toys. Sure enough, here was a train set, a nice wooden one, with blue and red carriages. Carefully, he took it from the sack and laid it beside Mr Potter's note.

Hamish Bigmore, sitting by his own fireside, was writing *his* note to Santa – except that, since he didn't believe in Santa, it was meant for his mother and father to read:

PRESENTS I WANT
by Hamish Bigmore

It covered seventeen pages.

Over in the windmill, Santa was looking anxiously out of the window, hoping to catch a glimpse of Mr Majeika's progress. 'How do you think he's getting on, Rudolph?' he asked nervously.

'Search me, sir,' answered Rudolph, 'But if pressed for an answer, sir, I would offer the opinion that he is, almost beyond the shadow of doubt, making an utter and complete mess of it.'

'Oh no,' groaned Santa, burying his head in his hands.

*

Mr Majeika left School Cottage and set off down the road on his tricycle. Being laden with presents, it was very difficult to steer, and turning a corner he found himself heading straight for a ditch.

Crash! And a very uncomfortable crash it was too, landing in the ditch with half a ton of presents on top of him. Somehow he managed

to scramble free and pack everything back on
to the trike. As he did so, he realized that he
was being watched.

P.C. Pluckley of the Bartyshire Constabulary
was standing in the road, leaning on his bicycle,
and watching him carefully, as if he were a
burglar or some other criminal. ''Ello, 'ello, 'ello,'

he said to Mr Majeika. 'Taking Santa's place, are we?'

'However did you guess?' asked Mr Majeika, wide-eyed.

'If you wouldn't mind waiting there a moment, sir,' said P.C. Pluckley, opening the door of a telephone box, and ringing up his sergeant. 'Pluckley to Z Victor One,' he said into the receiver. 'There's a funny chappy out 'ere tonight, Sarge.'

'Aha?' answered the Sergeant's voice. 'Not dressed in a red outfit with a white beard, is he?'

''Ow did you guess, Sarge?' asked P.C. Pluckley.

'Book 'im, Pluckley!'

'Yes, Sarge.'

But Mr Majeika, who had been listening outside the telephone box, flicked his tuft, and P.C. Pluckley found that, for the moment at least, he couldn't open the door.

Mr Majeika fled.

Hamish Bigmore was just putting the
finishing touches to his list of presents. His
mother came into the kitchen. 'Come along,
Hamie, time for bed. You mustn't be awake
when Santa comes.'

'Santa Claus!' scoffed Hamish. 'Haven't I told
you there's no such person?'

'But I definitely heard a noise in the chimney
just now,' said Pam. 'Oh well, Hamie darling,
don't be too long. Nighty night.'

Pamela Bigmore was perfectly right. There
had been a noise in the chimney. At that very
moment, Mr Majeika was struggling along the
Bigmore rooftop.

In the kitchen, Hamish thought of five more
presents he wanted. Suddenly there was a distant
cry, followed by the sound of something falling.

114

And then, coming from the fireplace: 'Help! Help!'

Hamish went over to the fireplace to listen more closely. 'Is anyone there?' he called.

'Yes!' answered the voice. 'I'm stuck!' Mr Majeika was indeed stuck, wedged half way down the Bigmores' chimney. Then he remembered that he was supposed to be Santa Claus. 'I bet you can't guess who I am, Hamish,' he said in a gruff voice that was meant to sound like Santa's.

'Of course I can,' answered Hamish. 'You're a burglar!'

'No, no!' called Mr Majeika hastily. 'I'm Santa Claus!'

But Hamish had already hurried to the telephone, to call the Much Barty Police.

The Carol Singers had just reached the
Bigmore house and struck up 'God Rest Ye
Merry Gentlemen' when Hamish ran out
excitedly. 'Guess who I've got stuck up my
chimney!' he shouted. 'A burglar who says he's
Santa Claus!'

Thomas and Melanie looked anxiously at
one another, then up at the roof of the Bigmore
house. Sure enough, there were Mr Majeika's
legs sticking out of a chimney pot, waving
desperately in the air.

'Come on!' gasped Melanie. 'There's no time
to lose!' Even as they ran off, they could hear
the police car approaching.

At the windmill, Santa was biting his nails anxiously. 'Still no sign of him flying across the sky, Rudolph?' he asked.

'I fear not, sir,' answered Rudolph. 'Indeed, it appears that he is in trouble. The Smalls are running back here across the field.'

'It's Mr Majeika!' panted Thomas and Melanie when they reached the windmill. 'He's stuck in a chimney!'

'It seems to me, sir,' said Rudolph, 'that the time has come for you to Save The Situation, sir.'

'Don't look at me, Rudolph,' gasped Santa. 'You know I'd give anything to be back there in the sky with my sleigh, but it's broken in pieces, and as to the flying, I've completely lost my nerve.'

'The sleigh is once again in working order, sir,' said Rudolph gravely. 'I myself have performed the necessary repairs while you, sir, if I may say so, have been blithering around. And as to your famous fear of heights, sir, I

think that Thomas and I, with the aid of Mr
Majeika's collection of Walpurgian apothecary
bottles, might be able to concoct something
that would do the trick, eh, Thomas?'

'You mean a home-made Flying Potion?'
asked Thomas excitedly. 'You bet. Let's get on
with it, Rudolph!'

The police car had drawn up outside the
Bigmore house, and the Carol Singers followed
Hamish and the two policemen into the
kitchen.

'There he is, men!' Hamish told the police,
pointing at the fireplace. 'Go in and get him!'

What Hamish did not know was that, at
that moment, Mr Majeika had remembered an
old Walpurgian spell for freeing yourself from

tight places. A flick of his tuft, and he was out of the chimney. He sat on the roof panting for breath, and cleaning the soot off his Santa Claus clothes.

The police sergeant was peering up the chimney. 'Come on out with your hands up,' he called into it. But there was silence. He

peered again. 'Wait a minute,' he said. 'I can see the moonlight up there. The chimney's not blocked. There's no one in it. You've been pulling our legs, haven't you, Master Bigmore?'

Mr Majeika was just wondering if he had the nerve to climb off the Bigmores' roof when he heard a jingling, and to his astonishment, saw Santa's sleigh gliding across the village rooftops. Santa himself was driving it, and Thomas and Melanie were on board. 'Mr Majeika!' they called. 'We've come to rescue you!'

A few moments later, P.C. Pluckley and the Sergeant were leaving the Bigmore house, in a very bad temper at having their time wasted.

The Sergeant had told Hamish Bigmore what he thought about small boys who called out the police as a hoax. Now Bunty Brace-Girdle, Mr Potter, and the rest of the Carol Singers were telling Hamish the same thing, and for once, Hamish had been reduced to silence.

As they came out of the front door, the two policemen glanced into the sky. They blinked, and looked at one another. 'Did you think you saw what *I* thought I saw, Pluckley?' asked the Sergeant.

'Two men with white beards and red clothes, and two children, flying across the sky in a sleigh, Sarge?'

'That's right, Pluckley. But we couldn't 'ave seen any such thing, could we, Pluckley? Must 'ave been those mince pies the Carol Singers gave us.' And they got into the police car and drove off.

Up in the sky, Melanie and Thomas were gazing down in wonder at the world beneath.

'Hold on tight, children,' called Santa. 'We've got a long journey ahead of us, and a long night delivering presents. Oh, I feel fine after that Flying Potion!'

'Trust a reindeer to sort things out, sir,' said Rudolph. 'Next time you're in trouble, you might think of asking me to take over your job . . . sir!'

Mr Majeika sighed. 'What's the matter?' the children asked him.

'I've just remembered,' he said, 'that I forgot to give you both a Christmas present.'

'Oh, but Mr Majeika,' said Thomas, 'but you did! You've given us a ride in Santa's sleigh, and that's the best present anyone could ever have.'

'You bet it is!' said Melanie. 'A happy Christmas, Mr Majeika!'

What's cooking in Walpurgis?

Perhaps you would like to try some of this wizard queasy-cuisine! It comes from Mr Majeika's own recipe book, which was written for him by his Aunty Bubbles, the best witch-cook in Walpurgis.

MUGWORT MORSELS – suitable for serving at Cauldron Cook-Ins. Take one freshly baked loaf, fill with squashed eggies, and stuff with dollops of cress. Then smother the outside in cream cheese, and decorate with tiny cut-out shapes of broomsticks and stars.

Makes 8 slices

1 unsliced wholemeal loaf

Softened butter (or low fat margarine)

2/3 hardboiled eggs, mashed

Cress

2 tablespoons mayonnaise

Ground black pepper (optional, for witches who
   like their food spicy)

For the outside slurp:

A carton of cream cheese

For the decorations:

$\frac{1}{2}$ green pepper

Cucumber skin

Chopped spring onions (optional)

Parsley

Remove the crust from the bread and slice horizontally into three pieces. Spread the butter on each piece. Mix eggs with mayonnaise and ground black pepper. Smother with cress, and make into a three-layer sandwich. Transfer to serving plate and smother in cream cheese (weight-watching witches beware!). Then decorate by carefully cutting all the green garnishes into broomstick and star shapes.

BATS' BLOOD SOUP – even tastier when eaten by moonlight! A delicious home-made soup, straight from the cauldron, topped with wizardy croutons.

Serves 4

1 onion, peeled and chopped (this'll make you cry!)

1 potato, peeled and chopped

3 tablespoons cooking oil

2 tablespoons tomato purée

2 lbs tomatoes, peeled and chopped (soak them in very hot water to make the skins come off)

$1\frac{1}{4}$ pints chicken stock (you can use a stock cube stirred into hot water)

A bayleaf, salt and black pepper (optional)

Slices of bread cut into wizard's hat shapes

*

Fry the onion and potato in the oil for five minutes. Stir in the tomato purée. Add chopped tomatoes, chicken stock, bayleaf and salt and pepper. Bring it to the boil, turn down the heat, and simmer for about 25 minutes. Remove the bayleaf, pour the soup into a liquidiser, and blend it till smooth. Fry the hat-shaped pieces of bread in butter or olive oil till they're golden brown and ready to float on the top of your cauldron.

STARRY NIGHT DELIGHTS – Star-shaped puff pastry savouries are even tastier when filled with your own favourite pâté.

For twenty stars, simply defrost a packet of puff pastry, roll it out, and cut into star shapes. Then brush with beaten egg, sprinkle some sesame seeds over them (they're crunchy!), and cook at gas mark 7 (220°C) for 5 minutes. Let them cool, split them horizontally, and fill with your favourite yummy pâté (vegetarians can use cream cheese or other non-meat fillings).

AND TO WASH IT ALL DOWN ...

AUNTY BUBBLES' BREW – It's what gives all Mr Majeika's witch-aunties that extra-special zest for dancing their Dance of the Seven Cobwebs, under a Walpurgian Waning Moon. It's deliciously simple, and best served chilled.

For one cool drink, take

$\frac{1}{4}$ pint plain yoghurt

$\frac{1}{4}$ pint cold milk

2 tablespoons Ribena or other blackcurrant cordial

Place the ingredients in your Aunty Bubbles blender, whirr up a storm till it's smooth, then pour into your very tallest glasses, and drink it down slowly to the very bewitching drop.

**BON APPÉTIT
SAYS AUNTY BUBBLES!**